7"
KARA
A COMIC BY BECCA HILLBURN

7"kara
Volume 1

Story and Art by
becca hillburn

Chapters 1 and 2 originally published as single issue copies in 2013.

Chapters 3 and 4 have never before seen publication of any sort, including digital, prior to the release of this volume.

Bonus story, "Small Blessings" first published in the shoujo anthology Hana Doki Kira (hanadokikira.tumblr.com) in 2014.

All chapters, though not the bonus material, syndicated on 7inchkara.com as a webcomic post-publication.

© 2013 Becca Hillburn
ISBN: 978-1-735567808
Editing and Critique/Alex Hoffman, Chris Paulsen, Heidi Black, Frankie Coleman, Joseph Coco
Design/Becca Hillburn
Layout/Heidi Black

The story, characters, and events depicted within this book are sadly entirely fictional.

Published by Nattosoup Studio
becca.hillburn@gmail.com
@nattosoup
nattosoup.com
Mailing list: nattosoup.com/artnerds

Dedication

This volume has a multi part dedication, in order of no particular importance.

This book is dedicated to Kara, because it is her story.

This book is dedicated to Midnite and Bowie, the joint inspiration for Pancake.

This book is dedicated to Joseph Coco, for reminding me that this story is worth telling, even when others insist that it is not.

This book is dedicated to my mother, Denise Hillburn, who read beautiful stories to me as a child and believes that children need good books.

TABLE OF CONTENTS

INTRODUCTION

Beneath a porch. In a forgotten attic. In a dusty shed. If you look carefully, you'll find Lilliputians, tiny people who live in the spaces humans have forgotten. Some call them 'littles'. Others 'thumblings'. A few may even know them as 'borrowers'.

Many cultures have stories about these tiny people. Some are good-natured and good luck, like the elves that helped the old cobbler. Some are mischievous, like the imps who play tricks on humans for amusement. The Lilliputians I've met fall somewhere in between, just like the humans I know. They exist for their own sakes, and for the most part, don't care much about humans. Tiny people have been with us since the beginning, we often simply fail to notice them.

This story is about Kara, a Lilliputian girl living with her parents in a neglected shed attached to a once-shuttered house. When a new human family moves into the house, Kara's life begins to expand and change. This volume contains the first four chapters of this ongoing watercolor comic, as well as a bonus story and concept art used in developing 7" Kara. I hope you'll enjoy it!

Kara
who is only
7" tall

Tanner
Kara's Friend

Naomi
A human girl

6

Important Characters

Rowan
Kara's Father

Meldina
Kara's Mother

Pancake
Naomi's kitten

OAK

GREEN PEAS

BLACKBERRIES

ROSES

STORAGE SHED

CHARCOAL GRILL

WORKSHOP SHED

PECAN TREE

BANANA TREES

BARTLETT PEAR

JAPANESE FIG

BIG HOUSE

BLUEBERRIES

CREPE MYRTLE

PECAN TREE

SOLD

PEACH TREE

10

11

13

18

Chapter 1 was completed in the winter of 2012, as a portion of the comic requirement for my Master's thesis. It was painted on Canson's Student paper, a product I do not revisit for later chapters.

Watercolor paper test. Spring 2013. Watercolor on Blick Studio Cold Press watercolor paper.

7" kara
Ch 2

CHAPTER 2
BECCA HILLBURN

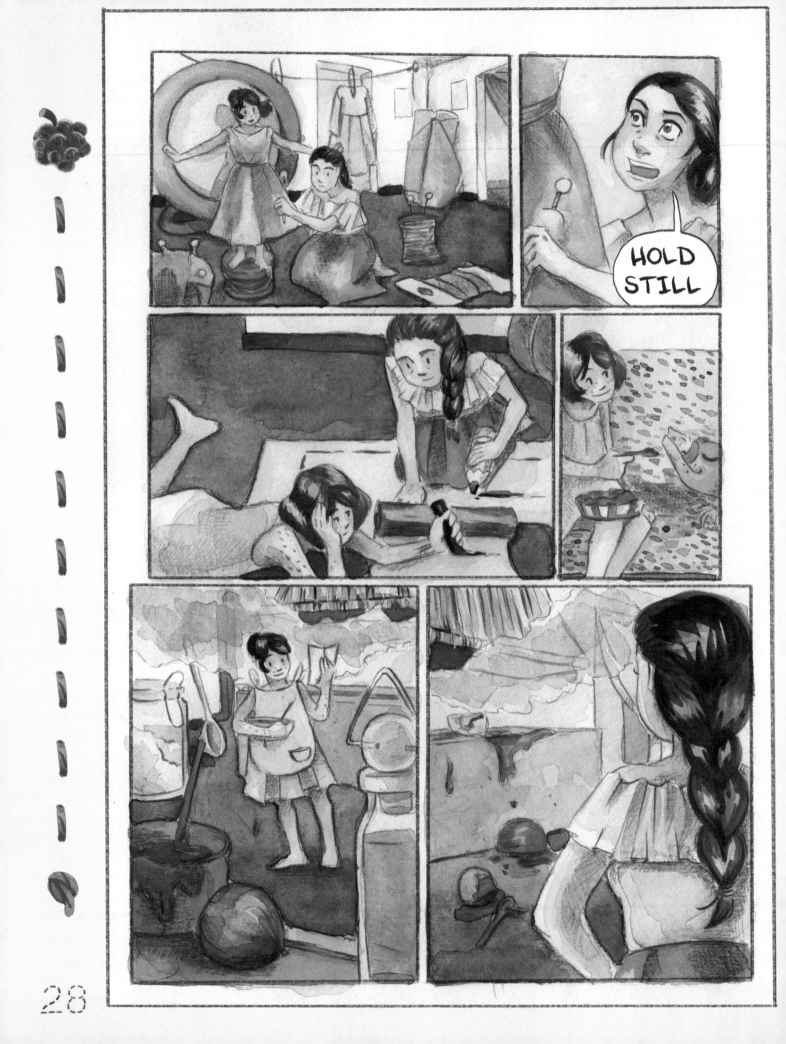

28

31

34

GO GET YOUR MOTHER...

35

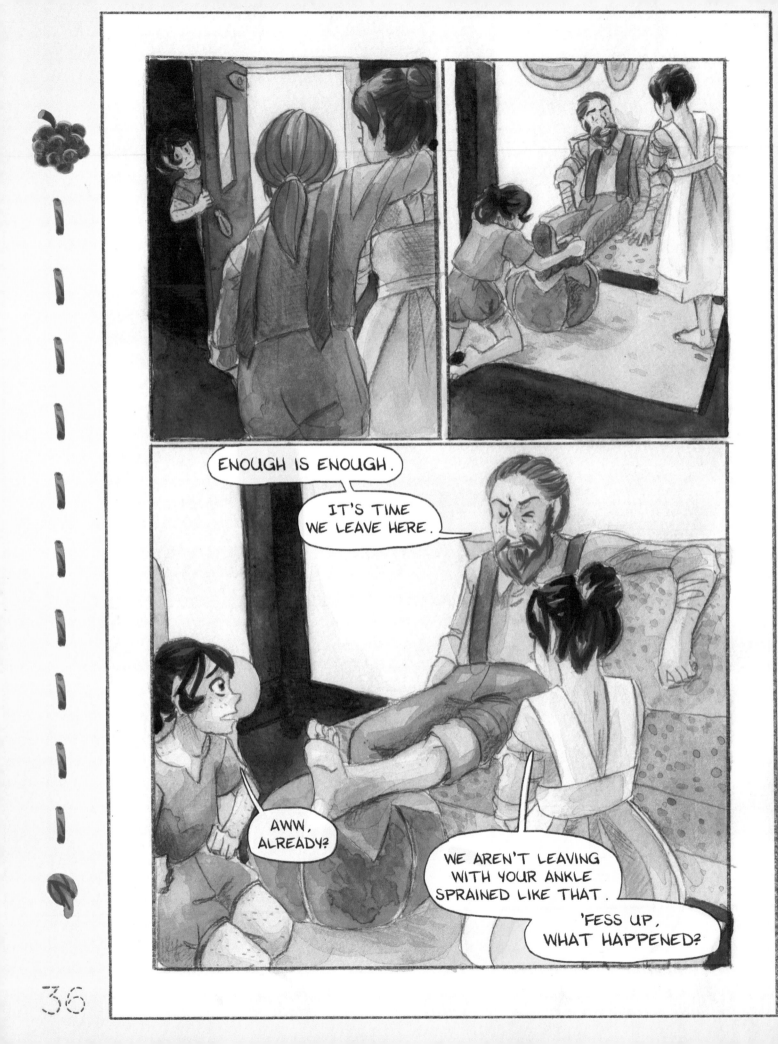

36

37

41

43

45

46

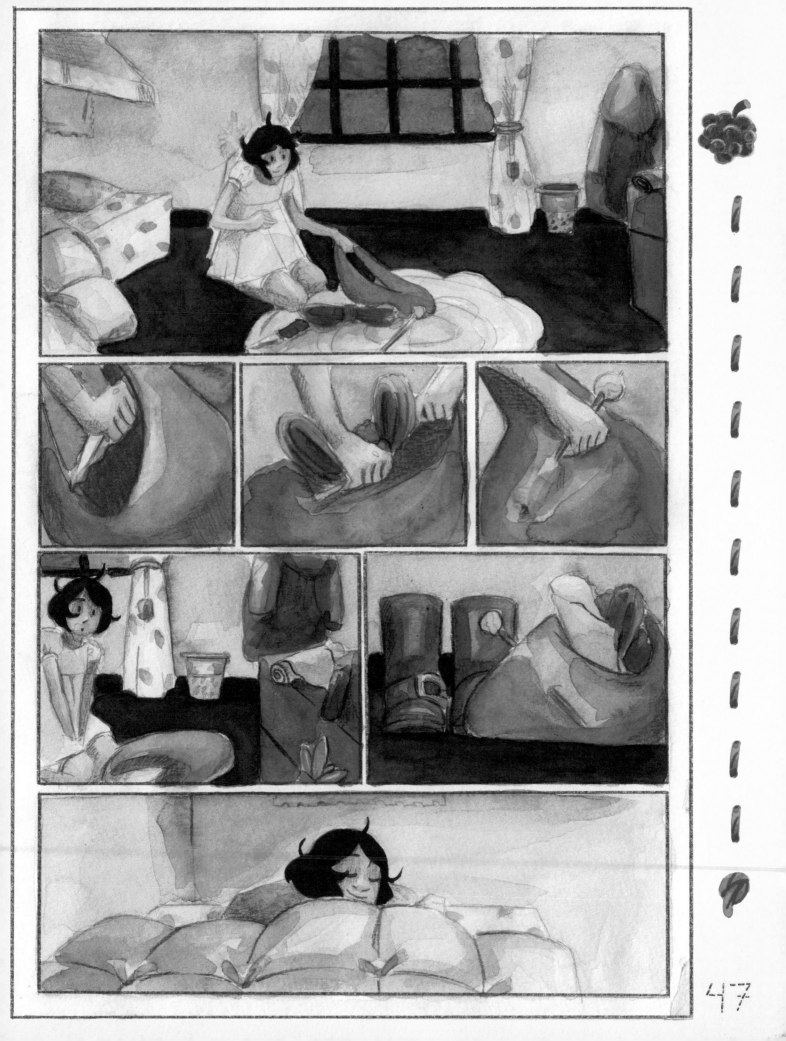

47

Chapter 2 completed the comics portion of my Master's thesis. Completed in Spring of 2013. Both Chapter 1 and Chapter 2 were debuted as single issue, full-color garage prints at MoCCA Fest 2013.

Shrinky Dink charm design. 2013. Digital.

49

"Play Your Tamborine for Me" 2013. Digital.

crunch!

rssstle

55

61

Chapter 3 was completed after my move from Savannah, GA to Nashville, TN, in the fall of 2013.

Kara with Tea Roses. 2014. Watercolor on Fluid Cold Press watercolor paper.

Watercolor test. Late 2012. Watercolor on Blick Studio Cold Press watercolor paper.

Ikara Ch.4

69

71

72

73

75

78

Chapter 4 was completed Late Winter 2014. Preparations for Volume 1 began shortly after.

Bonus Story
"Small Blessings"

This bonus story, "Small Blessings" was written and drawn for the shoujo comic anthology, Hana Doki Kira in 2013. While shoujo manga might be Japanese, Hana Doki Kira is an American anthology put together by the Year 85 group, a group of young women with a shoujo aesthetic to their comics. My own work falls into this category, and I was delighted to be asked to take part in this anthology. Although I did not have to contribute a Kara story, I wanted the opportunity to play around with a slightly different aesthetic. For this anthology, contributors were offered three colors to work with- black, white, and Pantone's Seafoam Green, as well as any gradients that resulted from the mixing of these hues. This was quite a departure from my usual full-spectrum range of watercolors, and presented a unique challenge that I was excited to tackle. For this comic, I altered the way I drew Kara slightly, and developed a wispier way of rendering lineart. I also tried to plan for the seafoam green halftone while preparing my pages.

The story itself is pretty simple. A younger Kara (around six or seven) finds an egg one day, and eagerly waits for it to hatch. I wanted a story that worked in pantomime, so even the youngest readers could follow along.

KARA

Rejected Title page for Volume 1. 2014. Watercolor on Cold Press Arches Paper

Kara

A sheltered 11 year old Lilliputian girl.

Original Kara Concept, 2010

Acorn loaf

Earring

Bit of Crumble

Pins

Shard of glass knife

blue berries

bobbin

string

belt pouch (magnified)

paper bark

charcoal

"What's in Kara's bag?" exercise, 2011

YEP!

VWEEEE!! vween~

ALOHA!

I feel strangely... energetic.

NYA

Prompted gesture studies for character development, 2011

Kara 'borrowing' exercises, 2012

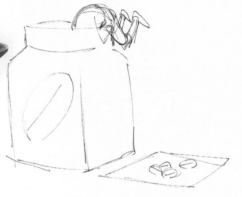

Marker mood and expression exercises,
2013

Kara marker exercise,
2014

(*≧ｍ≦*)   (ﾉﾉ#´Д｀)

｜≧Д≦｜

(¬‿¬)

(＾◡＾)

┌(･_･)┐

(⌒▽⌒)

ｒ(＾ω＾)

(￣◇￣;)

(`･ω･´)

(＾▽＾)

(TｰT)

@▽@

Kara expressions based on Japanese emoji, 2014

Rowan An over-protective patriarch.

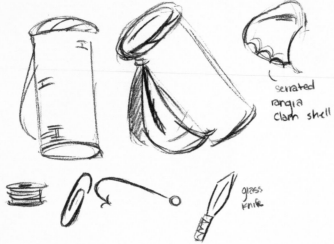

serrated
rangia
clam shell

glass
knife

Rowan's hunting and gathering gear is based off South American back packs. The contents vary, but he almost always carries a bobbin of thread or fishing line, a serrated rangia clam shell that serves as a handsaw, a fish hook, and a paper clip.

Height comparison chart between Meldina, Kara, and Rowan. 2012

Rowan revised concept, 2012.

Meldina

A dedicated mother and hard-working seamstress.

Ink sketch of Kara and her mother interacting. 2013

Dealing w/ a rapidly growing daughter on the cusp of puberty

Generally patient + kind

Screw-up around humans, can see the benefit of association

Wants to stick it out

Renowned seamstress

2840

Original Meldina concept, 2012

Kara's mom has pet spiders for silk thread can be woven

family things

Meldina harvests spider silk for thread and weaving. Concept, 2014

cheesecloth

Kara catches flies for the spider. Dusty, her gecko

fruit fly trap juice

Inked clothing study for Meldina. 2013

Pancake

A friendly kitten who finds all humans smell the same.

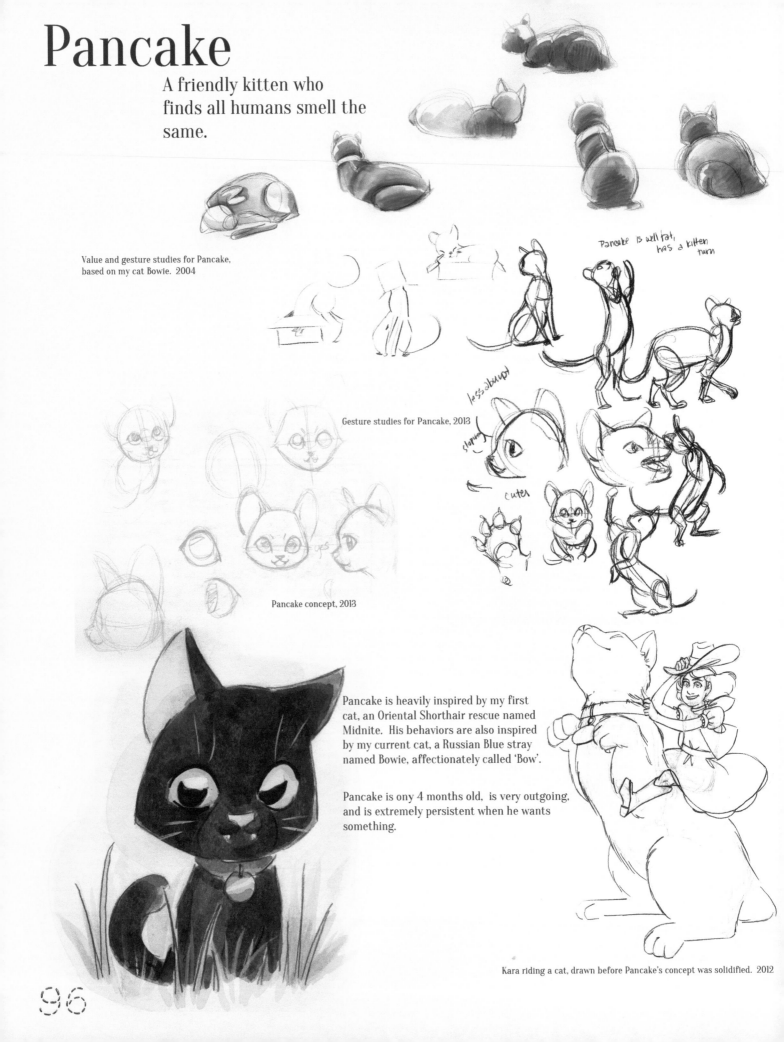

Value and gesture studies for Pancake, based on my cat Bowie. 2004

Pancake is well fat, has a kitten turn

Gesture studies for Pancake, 2013

less abrupt

slimmer

cuter

yes

Pancake concept, 2013

Pancake is heavily inspired by my first cat, an Oriental Shorthair rescue named Midnite. His behaviors are also inspired by my current cat, a Russian Blue stray named Bowie, affectionately called 'Bow'.

Pancake is ony 4 months old, is very outgoing, and is extremely persistent when he wants something.

Kara riding a cat, drawn before Pancake's concept was solidified. 2012

Naomi

A teenager caught between childhood and adulthood.

Naomi original concept, 2012

Naomi revised face, 2013

Naomi revised concept, 2013

Tanner

This messenger Lilliputian does not always bring good tidings.

Tanner original concept 2012

Tanner revised concept, 2013

Clothing concepts, 2012

Tanner and Kara interaction, 2013

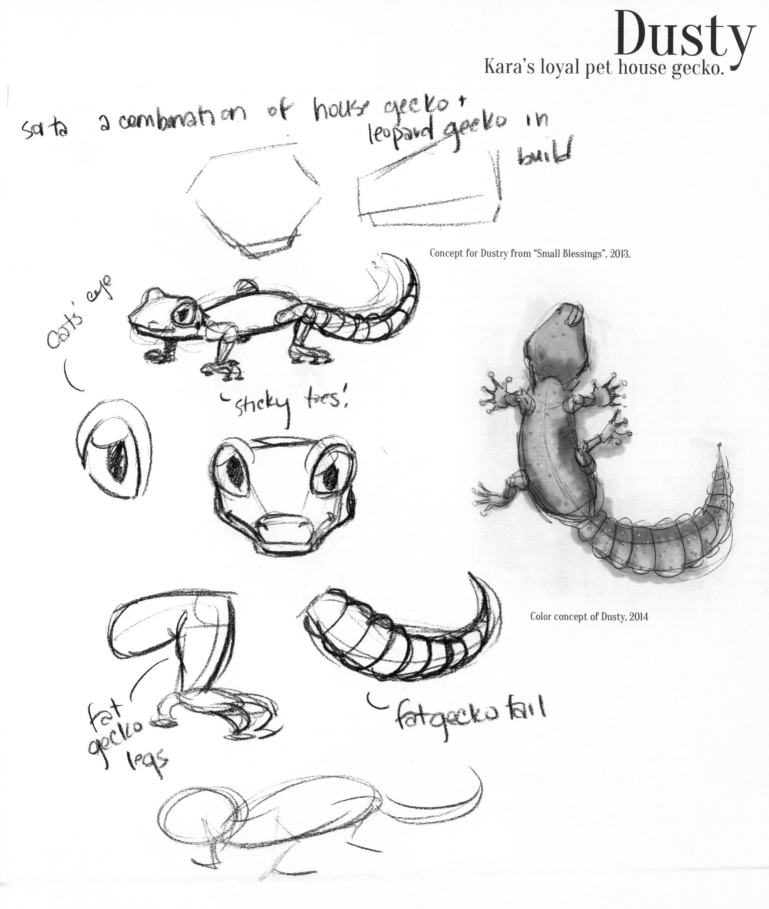

So ta a combination of house gecko + leopard gecko in build

Concept for Dustry from "Small Blessings", 2013.

cat's eye

'sticky toes!

Color concept of Dusty, 2014

fat gecko legs

fat gecko tail

Dusty is based on a combination of the house geckos found around my childhood home in Luling, Louisiana, and leopard geckoes commonly kept as pets. Dusty is very much modelled after my very fat leopard gecko, Clio.

Neighborhood Map

A typical (semi-fictional) neighborhood in Hahnville, Louisiana.

Although I've taken many liberties, the house and neighborhood in which this story are set are based on a real house and a small neighborhood, located in a small, rural town located on the west bank of the Mississippi River in south eastern Louisiana.

The real house belonged to my grandparents and was the house my mother grew up in. After my grandparents moved away, my aunt lived in the house. The backyard, in my experience, was almost always overgrown, and because my grandfather liked to tinker and repair things, there were two sheds stuffed full of treasures that the grandkids were not allowed to explore. As a kid who'd read *The Borrowers*, *The Littles*, *Stuart Little*, and *Gulliver's Travels*, I thought these sheds were the perfect place for little people to set up residence. Years later, when my aunt moved, my mother and I were in charge of cleaning out these sheds, which had gone untouched for decades. It was my experiences at this house that formed the nebulous framework for 7" Kara, many years ago.

Kara in the woods. Mood sketch. 2013.

Kara daily life elements.
From top: strawberry, black
berries, mushrooms, pecans,
acorn, button, violet flower,
sunflower seed, blueberry,
pine straw baskets, thimble,
thread with needle. 2012.

kara

Panel redraw from Chapter 2.
Kara and Meldin in storeroom,
opening jar of preserved fish.

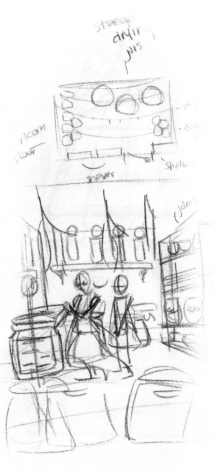

General Worldbuilding

A peek into a little world.

Kara arguing with her mother about having acorn mash for dinner. 2013.

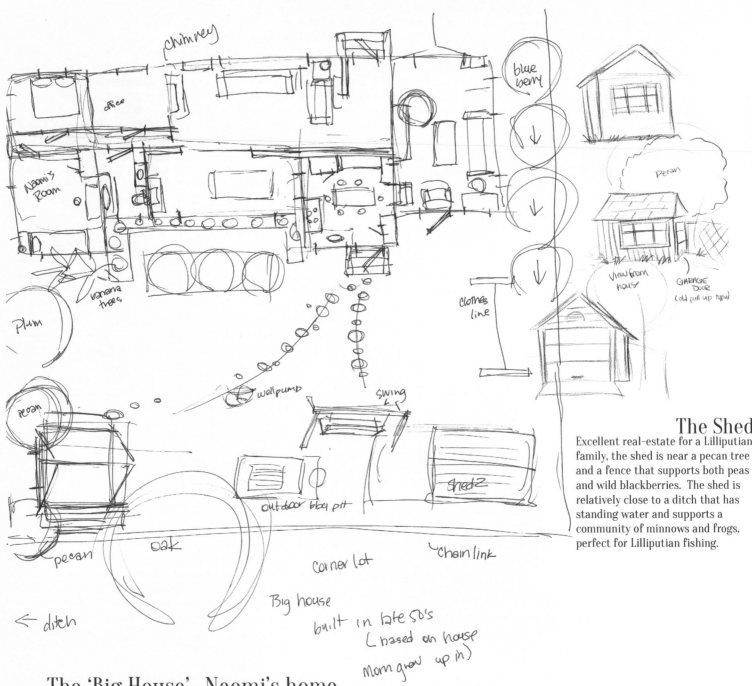

The labels within the sketch include: chimney, office, Naomi's Room, banana trees, Plum, pecan, ditch, oak, pecan, wellpump, outdoor bbq pit, swing, shed2, corner lot, chain link, clothes line, blue berry, Pecan, View from house, GARAGE DOOR (old pull up type), Big house built in late 50's (based on house Mom grew up in)

The Shed

Excellent real-estate for a Lilliputian family, the shed is near a pecan tree and a fence that supports both peas and wild blackberries. The shed is relatively close to a ditch that has standing water and supports a community of minnows and frogs, perfect for Lilliputian fishing.

The 'Big House'- Naomi's home.

At one time, this residence was the home to several Lilliputian families- two in the shed Kara's family occupies, two in the other shed, several beneath the house, a few in the attic. When the original owner's of the home passed away, the house set empty for several years, and all families but Meldina's parents moved away. The dollhouse has been in Meldina's family for two generations, and she's loathe to leave it just because a new human family has moved into the larger house.

The 'Big House', Shed, and Dollhouse

All the world Kara has ever known.

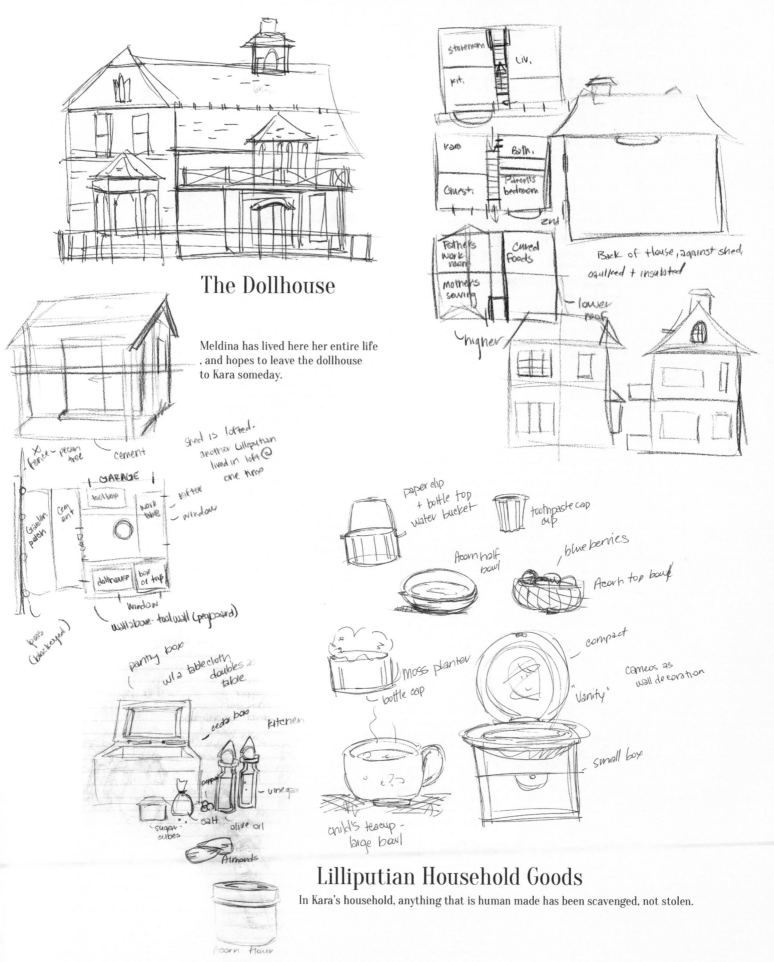

The Dollhouse

Meldina has lived here her entire life, and hopes to leave the dollhouse to Kara someday.

Lilliputian Household Goods

In Kara's household, anything that is human made has been scavenged, not stolen.

Inked Concept
At one time, Kara was going to be in black and white.

Kara carrying berries. 2012

Study for Chapter 1 cover, 2012

Kara, mood test, 2012

Kara, mood test, 2012

BECCA HILLBURN

CREATOR

About the Artist

Becca Hillburn is a children's comic artist from New Orleans, LA, who graduated from SCAD: The University for Creative Careers with a Master's Degree in Sequential Art (comics!) in 2013. She now resides in Destrehan, LA and enjoys the beautiful swamps. Becca firmly believes that little girls read comics. She may also believe that Lilliputians eat the cookies she leaves out, and that a Lilliputian family live beneath her back porch. Besides creating comics for girls, she blogs about comics, conventions, and art supplies, and attends a variety of conventions along the eastern American coast. For more of her comics, check out her blog and her online shop!

Email: becca.hillburn@gmail.com
Art Videos: youtube.com/nattosoup
Twitter / Instagram: @nattosoup
Mailing List: updates.7inchkara.com/comic
Blog: nattosoup.blogspot.com
Website: nattosoup.com

Thanks

Special thanks to Heidi Black for being so patient with me while I was laying out this book. A lot of the illustrations were actually completed while she was laying out pages. Her help in laying out this book made it possible for twice as much to be accomplished in the same amount of time.

And also to Joseph Coco who is not only my biggest supporter, but did a lot of editing at various stages of this book's completion, including later draft pdfs.

Thanks also to Chris Paulsen and Alex Hoffmann who heard a lot of venting during my creation of this book and didn't run to the hills screaming.

Lastly, thanks to all of you who've shown support for 7" Kara over the last year. Thanks for reblogging, retweeting, and signal boosting comic pages and individual illustrations.

Life as a Lilliputian means keeping lots of secrets, and Kara's biggest secret just keeps getting bigger, threatening to divide her family. Is this larger than life friendship really worth the risk?

7inchkara.com/volume2

CPSIA information can be obtained
at www.ICGtesting.com
Printed in the USA
LVHW071812011121
702137LV00002B/87